What a perfect way to bring a little San Francisco to my favorite Hammond kiddos!

xxo,
Jenny Hutsell
07/13

CLYDE
the Cable Car

by Ron Berman
Illustrations by Frank Hill

Clyde the Cable Car
Copyright ©2006
Ron Berman and Frank Hill

This book is distributed by:
Smith Novelty Co., San Francisco, California
888.861.7626   www.smithnovelty.com
United States Copyright Office #TXu 550 246 • 12.28.92

Printed In Korea

Clyde the Cable Car
was filled with pride.
Today was the day
for his very first ride.
He said, "I'll do it. Yes I will
I'll climb that San Francisco hill."

"I'll climb to the top
and make every stop.
I'll be the cream of
the Cable Car crop."

He knew he could be
the best he could be
picking up folks
from A to Z.

At every stop
from near to far,
Look who got on
the Cable Car!

Alfonse the arrogant Alligator going downtown to his job as a waiter.

Barkwell the Beagle,
a Mason Street pup.

Carrie the Crab
who was just cracking up.

Danforth the Duck,
a Nob Hill gent . . .

NO PARKING

and Ellie
the Elegant Elephant.

F

Felix the Fox
and his friends the Giraffes.

Huntington Hippo,
a ton of laughs.

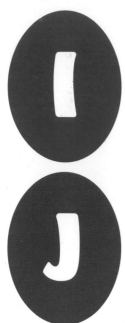

Izzy Iguana
was tipping his hat
to Jerry the Jaguar
a really cool cat.

Hopping aboard was
Kip Kangaroo
with Lion Cub Lisa
from the SF Zoo.

K

L

M

N

Manny the Monkey
saw Nell the Gnu.
"Hey, Gnu!
What's Gnu with you?"
(We know it's strange,
but it's plain to see
that Gnu doesn't start
with an N but a G.)

Olive the Ostrich
buried her head
in a basket of
North Beach
sour dough bread.

**Pierre the Pig
climbed on and sat down
with Queenie the Quail
from Chinatown.**

P

Q

KUNG FU LESSONS

Randolph Raccoon
jumped on and sat
next to Sally the Seal
who was having a chat

with Tara the Toucan
and her friend with a horn,
Una the Union Street Unicorn.

T

U

Vera the Vulture,
a very strange bird,
held hands with a Walrus –
they looked so absurd.

(There were no riders, at least one suspects, who had a name that starts with an X.)

At last,
a Yak who was from the Bahamas
jumped on with a Zebra
in black striped pajamas.

Said Clyde,
"I did it. I climbed to the top."
Then he clanged with joy and just
couldn't stop.

His passengers cheered
and jumped off to go . . .

and have a great day
in San Francisco.

They roamed the town
from morning till night.

They hardly sat down
except for a bite.

And on the way home, mile after mile,
all that Clyde could do was smile.

He just couldn't wait to tell Mom and Dad
of the wonderful ride their little boy had.

"I did it!" sang Clyde.
"Just little old me.
I'm filled with pride
from A to Z."